GROW FOR IT!

Journal

THROUGH THE SCRIPTURES

KATHY LYNN
DAVID LYNN
AND

_____ ___ ___ ___ _ _
YOUR NAME HERE

GROW FOR IT! *Journal* THROUGH THE SCRIPTURES

written by
Kathy Lynn
and David Lynn

illustrations by
Dan Pegoda

The spiritual journey of

_____

for the year _____

_____   _____
Date of First Entry   Date of Last Entry

Youth Specialties

Edited by Lorraine Triggs
Interior design and typography by Jack Rogers
Cover design by Jack Rogers

Printed in the United States of America

0-310-49031-6

96 97 98 99 /CH/ 10 9 8 7 6 5 4

GROW FOR IT! Journal THROUGH THE SCRIPTURES

Welcome to **Grow-For-It Journal through the Scriptures.** Like the original **Grow-For-It Journal**, this is a journal that *you* will write. You will be taking a journey through the Bible, recording your thoughts and feelings. This volume lets you take a look at real Bible characters who had real problems. You can examine their lives and concerns and compare them to your own. You may be surprised to learn that the Bible is full of real people like yourself. And just as you can, they turned to God for help and guidance.

Before you begin this journey, let us explain a few things. First, a journal is not a diary. A diary is a random or unstructured account of your days. A journal, on the other hand, is a structured account, and this journal is structured to help you grow spiritually as you investigate Bible stories and passages. This journal contains fifty-two activities, some of which will take more than one day. The important thing is that you see each of the activities as a suggestion. Feel free to change the activities any way you want. Following each activity is an "extra credit" exercise, which can help you focus on the spiritual implications of each of the Bible story or passage activities. Use this exercise before, during, or after each journal activity. The Scriptures and questions you find there can help get you thinking.

One more comment about the journal activities. We've put them in order of their appearance in the Bible (except for the "Popular Bible Passages" and "Living the Psalms"), but you, of course, are welcome to skip around. Also, you can choose to write in your journal on a daily or a weekly basis. The important thing is that you write *regularly.* Growth—whether it's physical, mental, or spiritual—is constant. It's always happening even though we can't see it, and that's why it's important to write regularly. You'll be surprised to look back at your words and see what was happening even when you felt as if nothing was going on in your life. You can also keep track of major life events and prayer requests on the pages in the back of the book.

Finally, keep your journal in a private place. Read it periodically and reflect on what you have written. Your past descriptions of your thoughts and feelings will be effective reminders of where you have been and, more importantly, of just how far you've come.

Now you can Grow For It—through the Scriptures!

Kathy Lynn
David Lynn

HELPFUL HINTS

1. Set aside the same time each day or week to write. Make it a permanent and regular part of your schedule. Make the personal commitment not to let anything get in the way of your writing time.

2. Don't force words to come. And don't worry about how good the words sound. Just write what comes to mind. You don't have to use perfect grammar or complete sentences. Remember that this is a record of *your* thoughts and feelings; however you communicate these things is okay!

3. Remember to date all of your writings so that when you reread your journal, you'll know exactly when you wrote a specific entry.

4. Write clearly and legibly so that you can read what you write for years to come.

5. Find a safe and private place to keep your journal. This book is for you to read. It is not for other people to see unless you choose to share it.

TABLE ◆ OF
CONTENTS

28. THE DEVIL MADE ME DO IT Matthew 4:1-11 _____

29. LIVING THE PSALMS #3 Psalms 8; 65; 96; 100; 117; 150 _____

30. SMART BUILDING Matthew 7:24-27 _____

31. HOW'S YOUR EYESIGHT? Matthew 14:22-33 _____

32. JESUS STORY #3 Matthew 16:21-23 _____

33. JESUS HAD A LITTLE LAMB Matthew 18:12-14 _____

34. PRAYER STORY #4 Mark 14:32-42 _____

35. JESUS WHO? Mark 14:66-72 _____

36. GOOD SAM Luke 10:25-37 _____

37. POPULAR PASSAGES #4 Jeremiah 17:7, 8; Romans 12:13; Galatians 5:22, 23; Philippians 4:6, 7; James 4:7 _____

38. A FOOL AND HIS MONEY Luke 12:13-21 _____

39. NIGHT QUEST John 3:1-21 _____

40. LIVING THE PSALMS #4 Psalms 23; 63; 86; 116; 139 _____

41. A FAMOUS DOUBTER John 20:24-29 _____

42. LET'S REVIEW #2 Acts 7:2-50; 7:51-53 _____

43. PERSECUTION PLUS Acts 8:1-4 _____

44. POPULAR PASSAGES #5 Micah 6:8; John 14:27; Romans 13:14; Philippians 1:6; 2 Timothy 2:22 _____

45. PROBLEM-FREE Acts 9:23-26 _____

46. JESUS STORY #4 Acts 10:39-43 _____

47. GET RID OF THE "DIS" IN DISAGREEMENT Acts 15:35-40 _____

48. IN LOVE WITH THE WORLD 2 Timothy 4:9,10 _____

49. LET'S REVIEW #3 Hebrews 11 _____

50. A CHANGE OF HEART Jude 3 and 4 _____

51. POPULAR PASSAGES #6 John 16:33; Romans 12:9; 1 Corinthians 10:31; Galatians 2:20; 1 Peter 5:7 _____

52. THE END _____

ONE

THE WAY THINGS USED TO BE

If you've watched the news lately, you know the world is messed up. Even if you haven't caught the news, you know that things could be better. The world was not always in such bad shape. Read the Creation story found in Genesis 2:4-25 to get a picture of the way things used to be.

Which of the following do you think God wanted in His creation? (Check all those that apply.)

___ pollution
___ dishonesty
_X_ friendship
___ beauty
_X_ responsibility
___ violence
___ discrimination
_X_ caring
___ anxiety
_X_ peace
_X_ love
___ fear

Why did God want the best for His creation?

Why does God want the best for you?

How can you have God's best for your life?

DATE COMPLETED: _8-27-97_

EXTRA ☑ CREDIT

"You are worthy, our Lord and God, to receive glory and honor and power,
for you created all things, and by your will they were created
and have their being."
Revelation 4:11

God created people because He wanted them to glorify and enjoy Him. Make a list of all of the ways you enjoy God right now.

Name the things that are keeping you from enjoying God right now.

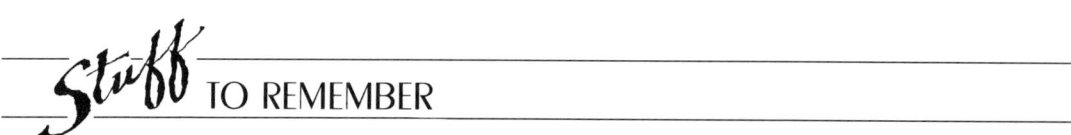

Stuff TO REMEMBER

Write down one thing you want to remember about today.

Today's date: _____

TWO

JESUS STORY #1

The Gospel story begins right after Adam and Eve sinned. In the midst of this sad story of sin, there was hope. God vowed to crush Satan. A Savior was promised! You can read about it in Genesis 3:1-15.

Make a list of all the words you think of when you hear the word "sin." Here are a few to get you started:

rebellion
falling short
guilt

Now make a list of all the words God thinks of when He considers your sin. Again, here are a few to help you get started:

grace
forgiveness
confession

DATE COMPLETED: _____

E X T R A  C R E D I T

"As far as the east is from the west,
so far has he removed our transgressions from us."
Psalm 103:12

How do you feel when you consider this passage on forgiveness?

Stuff TO REMEMBER

Write down one thing you want to remember about today.

Today's date: _____

THREE
CHOICES AND CHALLENGES

Do you remember the story of Lot and his family? They ran for their lives before God destroyed the city in which they lived (see Genesis 19:1-26). Lot put himself in a bad situation by the choices he made before he ever moved to the wicked city of Sodom. You can read about those choices in Genesis 13:8-13.

Have you ever made choices without thinking of the consequences?

___ YES   ___ NO

What happened?

How does thinking about consequences help you make better choices?

DATE COMPLETED: _____

EXTRA ☑ CREDIT

"Do not be deceived: God cannot be mocked.
A man reaps what he sows."
Galatians 6:7

How can this verse help you make good choices?

Stuff TO REMEMBER

Write down one thing you want to remember about today.

Today's date: _____

FOUR

WHAT A FAMILY!

Family problems are not new. You can read about them in the first book of the Bible. Take a look at one family's situation in Genesis 37:12-36.

Now write down steps you can take to make your family life better.

My personal family improvement steps will be . . .

DATE COMPLETED: _____

EXTRA ☑ CREDIT

"Be completely humble and gentle; be patient,
bearing with one another in love."
Ephesians 4:2

If you practiced this Bible verse every day with your family, what might happen?

Stuff TO REMEMBER

Write down one thing you want to remember about today.

Today's date: _____

FIVE

POPULAR PASSAGES #1

Read each of the Bible passages listed below. Choose the one that you feel would be the most helpful for you today.

- ❏ Deuteronomy 32:3, 4
- ❏ Ecclesiastes 3:1-8
- ❏ Matthew 11:28
- ❏ Romans 5:3, 4
- ❏ 1 John 4:19

Now that you've made a choice . . .

1. Pray that the Holy Spirit will speak to you as you study the passage.
2. Read the passage over three more times.
3. Decide what the author of the passage was trying to teach the readers of the time.
4. Determine how the passage applies to you.
5. Write down any changes you'll make because of what you learned from studying the passage.

DATE COMPLETED: _____

E X T R A ☑ C R E D I T

"But as for you, continue in what you have learned and have become convinced of,
because you know those from whom you learned it, and how from infancy
you have known the holy Scriptures, which are able to make you wise for salvation
through faith in Christ Jesus."
2 Timothy 3:14, 15

What does studying the Scriptures do for you?

 TO REMEMBER

Write down one thing you want to remember about today.

Today's date: _____

SIX

NOT GOOD ENOUGH

One of the greatest people in the Bible felt inadequate. Moses didn't feel he was good enough to do what God had asked him to do. Read Moses' story in Exodus 3:1-15.

What do you do when you feel inadequate?

a. Put myself down.

b. Pray a lot.

c. Get depressed.

d. Call a friend.

e. Party.

f. Listen to music.

g. Talk with my parents.

h. Hang out by myself.

i. Other: _____

Describe when you feel the most like Moses.

DATE COMPLETED: _____

21

EXTRA ☑ CREDIT

*"Even to your old age and gray hairs I am he, I am he who will sustain you.
I have made you and I will carry you; I will sustain you and I will rescue you."*
Isaiah 46:4

"I am the Lord, the God of all mankind. Is anything too hard for me?"
Jeremiah 32:27

*"Indeed, the very hairs of your head are all numbered. Don't be afraid;
you are worth more than many sparrows."*
Luke 12:7

How can these verses comfort you when you feel inadequate?

 TO REMEMBER

Write down one thing you want to remember about today.

Today's date: _____

SEVEN
GIVE ME TEN

The Ten Commandments. You've heard these again and again. Everyone needs to hear them one more time. Before you read the Ten Commandments in Exodus 20:1-17, list as many as you can below:

1.
2.
3.
4.
5.
6.
7.
8.
9.
10.

How does keeping the Ten Commandments protect you and benefit your life?

DATE COMPLETED: _____

EXTRA ☑ CREDIT

"To the Jews who had believed him, Jesus said,
'If you hold to my teaching, you are really my disciples.
Then you will know the truth, and the truth will set you free.'"
John 8:31, 32

How does living out the teachings of Jesus help you?

 TO REMEMBER

Write down one thing you want to remember about today.

Today's date: _____

LIVING THE PSALMS #1

Choose one of these four psalms below. Circle it. Read it. Describe how you could put what this psalm says into practice in your life.

Psalm 1

Psalm 23

Psalm 37

Psalm 112

I could put this psalm into practice by . . .

DATE COMPLETED: _____

E X T R A ☑ C R E D I T

*"Do not let this Book of the Law depart from your mouth;
meditate on it day and night, so that you may be careful to do
everything written in it. Then you will be prosperous and successful."*
Joshua 1:8

How can living the Christian faith make you successful?

 TO REMEMBER

Write down one thing you want to remember about today.

Today's date: _____

NINE

YOUR GOLDEN CALF

When the people of Israel hadn't heard from God in forty days, they decided to make their own god. Read the story found in Exodus 32:1-4. How are you sometimes like the people of Israel?

In the space below, think of steps you can take to handle the tough times when you don't feel close to God.

DATE COMPLETED: _____

EXTRA  CREDIT

"The Lord is near to all who call on him,
to all who call on him in truth."
Psalm 145:18

Why might you have trouble believing that God is always near to you?

Stuff TO REMEMBER

Write down one thing you want to remember about today.

Today's date: _____

GRUMBLING INSTEAD OF GRATITUDE

The Lord rescued the Israelites from brutal slavery in Egypt; He then parted the waters of the Red Sea so that the people of Israel could escape the armies chasing them. The Lord provided water in the desert when His people were thirsty. The Lord guided the children of Israel with a cloud by day and fire by night. The Lord provided food, free food, for His people. And the people complained: "We want steak!" (or something like that). Read about their grumbling in Numbers 11:4-9.

Can you name a time you grumbled when you should have been grateful?

What happens when you are grateful?

How can you be more grateful for what God has done for you?

DATE COMPLETED: _____

E X T R A ☑ C R E D I T

"Always giving thanks to God the Father for everything,
in the name of our Lord Jesus Christ."
Ephesians 5:20

"Give thanks in all circumstances, for this is God's will for you in Christ Jesus."
1 Thessalonians 5:18

What keeps you from being grateful?

Describe a time it was hard for you to give thanks. Why was it hard to be grateful?

Make a list of ten things for which you are grateful:
1.
2.
3.
4.
5.
6.
7.
8.
9.
10.

Stuff TO REMEMBER

Write down one thing you want to remember about today.

Today's date: _____

LET'S REVIEW #1

Moses often took the Israelites to school to review what God had done for them. But the children of Israel were not always the best students. They quickly forgot about God's goodness, love, mercy, and holiness. Moses reminded them of God by reviewing what God had done for them in the past. Pick one of these story repeats and read it for yourself:

- Deuteronomy 4:32-40
- Deuteronomy 7:7-21
- Deuteronomy 8:1-5
- Deuteronomy 9:7—10:13
- Deuteronomy 11:1-7
- Deuteronomy 24:17, 18

Why did Moses continually remind the Israelites of what God had done for them?

Why do you think the people had such short memories of God's miracles?

How are you like or unlike the children of Israel?

Why is it easy to forget the good things God has done for you?

What are some things God has done for you that you need to remember?

DATE COMPLETED: _____

EXTRA ☑ CREDIT

"For I do not want you to be ignorant of the fact, brothers, that our forefathers were all under the cloud and that they all passed through the sea. . . . Now these things occurred as examples to keep us from setting our hearts on evil things as they did."
1 Corinthians 10:1, 6

Delivered from slavery in Egypt! Guided by a cloud! Escaped on dry land through the middle of the Red Sea! Paul gives a history lesson by highlighting a famous Bible story just as Moses had so often done. Paul points out that these history stories were recorded in the Bible for a purpose.

How can reviewing Bible stories help you live the Christian life?

What is one story from the Bible that has helped you? How has it helped you?

 TO REMEMBER

Write down one thing you want to remember about today.

Today's date: _____

TWELVE

BUILT UP

Everyone needs encouragement. The people in the Bible were no different. They felt defeated, lonely, hurt, and afraid. Moses understood this when he encouraged Joshua. You can read Moses' encouraging words in Deuteronomy 31:7, 8.

How do other people encourage you?

They Tell ~~Me what~~ what's good

Why is it encouraging to know that the Lord "will never leave you nor forsake you"? (Deuteronomy 31:8)

DATE COMPLETED: _____

EXTRA ☑ CREDIT

"And let us consider how we may spur one another on toward love and good deeds. Let us not give up meeting together, as some are in the habit of doing, but let us encourage one another—and all the more as you see the Day approaching."
Hebrews 10:24, 25

How does your involvement in church encourage you?

How might your involvement encourage others?

Stuff TO REMEMBER

Write down one thing you want to remember about today.

Today's date: _____

PRAYER STORY #1

If you remember the story of Gideon in the Old Testament, you'll recall that God's people, the Israelites, were being oppressed by their enemies. The Jews were in trouble and they cried out to God. Gideon helped defeat these enemies. You can read about their desperate situation and their desperate cry in Judges 6:1-6.

Rate your prayer life on the scale below.

| | | | | | | | | | | |

I only pray when
I am in trouble.

I pray consistently
regardless of my
circumstances.

How can you discipline yourself to pray more?

How can you discipline yourself to pray at times other than when you need help?

DATE COMPLETED: _____

EXTRA ✔ CREDIT

"And pray in the Spirit on all occasions with all kinds of prayers and requests.
With this in mind, be alert and always keep on praying for all the saints."
Ephesians 6:18

"Be joyful always; pray continually; give thanks in all circumstances,
for this is God's will for you in Christ Jesus."
1 Thessalonians 5:16-18

What does it mean in your life to pray all kinds of prayers and requests and pray continually?

 TO REMEMBER

Write down one thing you want to remember about today.

Today's date: _____

HEARING PROBLEMS

Why can't God talk to me in a voice I can actually hear? How can I know what God wants me to do? Why would God want to talk to me? Questions like these are asked by many Christians. As a young man, Samuel, who became an Old Testament prophet, was confused when God first spoke to him. His story is in 1 Samuel 3:1-10. After reading Samuel's story, complete these three sentences.

I am like Samuel when I . . .

I want God's guidance in my life because . . .

The one thing that might stand in the way of my hearing God speak to me is . . .

DATE COMPLETED: _____

E X T R A ☑ C R E D I T

"I will instruct you and teach you in the way you should go;
I will counsel you and watch over you."
Psalm 32:8

God promised to guide us. One way in which He guides today is through the Bible.
Look up each of the following passages. Next to each verse, write what God's Word
has to say to you.

Proverbs 3:5, 6 _____

_____

Luke 6:31 _____

_____

Romans 12:2 _____

_____

Philippians 4:8 _____

_____

Stuff TO REMEMBER

Write down one thing you want to remember about today.

Today's date: _____

FIFTEEN
ARMED AND DANGEROUS

David and Goliath. Five stones, a slingshot, faith in God, and a giant comes falling down. What an amazing story! You can read about it in 1 Samuel 17:1-54. Everyone faces Goliaths in their lives. Goliaths can be those people or things that keep you from serving God, or perhaps everyday problems.

Write a brief story here about the "Goliaths" that trouble your life.

DATE COMPLETED: _____

39

EXTRA ☑ CREDIT

*"So do not fear, for I am with you; do not be dismayed, for I am your God. I will
strengthen you and help you; I will uphold you with my righteous right hand."*
Isaiah 41:10

How can God's power working in you help you overcome those things in your life
that are defeating you?

 TO REMEMBER

Write down one thing you want to remember about today.

Today's date: _____

SIXTEEN

POPULAR PASSAGES #2

Read each of the Bible passages listed below. Choose the one that you feel would be the most helpful for you today.

- ❑ Ephesians 4:26
- ❑ Philippians 4:13
- ❑ 1 Timothy 4:12
- ❑ 2 Peter 3:9
- ❑ 1 John 4:1

Now that you've made a choice . . .

1. Pray that the Holy Spirit will speak to you as you study the passage.
2. Read the passage over three more times.
3. Decide what the author of the passage was trying to teach the readers of the time.
4. Determine how the passage applies to you.
5. Write down any changes you'll make because of what you learned from studying the passage.

DATE COMPLETED: _____

E X T R A ☑ C R E D I T

"Your word is a lamp to my feet and a light for my path."
Psalm 119:105

This verse sounds nice, but what does it mean in your life?

 TO REMEMBER

Write down one thing you want to remember about today.

Today's date: _____

SEVENTEEN

AT YOUR SERVICE

David and Jonathan were super close friends. You can read about their friendship in 1 Samuel 20:12-17. Here's a portrait of two friends who were willing to support and care about each other. Take a look at one of your friendships.

Choose one friend and write his or her name here: _____

THE BEST FOR YOUR FRIEND

Write down some examples of how you want the best for your friend.

(Example: I don't want him to drink at parties.)

_____
_____
_____
_____
_____
_____
_____

THE BEST FOR YOU

Write down some examples of how your friend has wanted the best for you.

(Example: She encouraged me when I flunked a math test.)

_____
_____
_____
_____
_____
_____
_____

Take a minute and pray about your friendships.

Are you making good friendship choices? If not, how can you start to make better ones?

DATE COMPLETED: _____

EXTRA ☑ CREDIT

"If one falls down, his friend can help him up.
But pity the man who falls and has no one to help him up!"
Ecclesiastes 4:10

Describe a time you helped a friend during a tough situation.

How did God work through this situation?

Stuff TO REMEMBER

Write down one thing you want to remember about today.

Today's date: _____

NINETEEN

LIVING THE PSALMS #2

There are seven psalms that focus on being truly
sorry for your sin—in a word, repentance.
All of us have sinned—and need to ask
for God's forgiveness. Select one of
the seven psalms listed below.
Read it, and then describe what
you learned about repentance.

- Psalm 32
- Psalm 38
- Psalm 51
- Psalm 102
- Psalm 130
- Psalm 143

I learned that . . .

DATE COMPLETED: _____

EXTRA ☑ CREDIT

"I, even I, am he who blots out your transgressions,
for my own sake, and remembers your sins no more."
Isaiah 43:25

"If we confess our sins, he is faithful and just
and will forgive us our sins and purify us from all unrighteousness."
1 John 1:9

God has forgiven you! How can you experience God's forgiveness in your life?

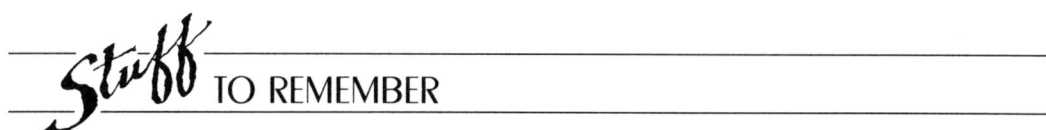 TO REMEMBER

Write down one thing you want to remember about today.

Today's date: _____

TWENTY

THE POOR-ME SYNDROME

The great prophet Elijah had his down times too! You can read about one of them in 1 Kings 19:1-10. After a great victory in his life, he started feeling sorry for himself. In spite of his fears, God worked in Elijah's life.

Check the five most helpful things from this list that you could do to allow God to work in your life when you are feeling down.

❑ Spend time alone with God in prayer, thinking about all the ways He loves you.

❑ Call a trustworthy friend to ask for support.

❑ Talk with your parents about what is bothering you.

❑ Look to the Scriptures for help.

❑ Have a long talk with God.

❑ Talk with your youth worker or pastor.

❑ Jog, walk, swim, or work out.

❑ Listen to your favorite music.

❑ Take a nap.

❑ Make a list of all the things for which you are grateful.

❑ Write your own: _____

DATE COMPLETED: _____

EXTRA ☑ CREDIT

"I sought the Lord, and he answered me;
he delivered me from all my fears."
Psalm 34:4

Many people turn away from God when they feel down. How can you turn to God rather than away from Him during the tough times?

 TO REMEMBER

Write down one thing you want to remember about today.

Today's date: _____

THE UNNAMED GIRL

A young girl captured and placed in slavery. It wasn't fair! She was torn from her family and friends. Yet her faith in God led her to share God's love with her captors. Read the story in 2 Kings 5:1-5.

Write a paragraph with one of these two sentences:

I could live like this young girl at my school, because . . .

I could not live like this young girl at my school, because . . .

DATE COMPLETED: _____

EXTRA ☑ CREDIT

*"You have heard that it was said, 'Love your neighbor and hate your enemy.'
But I tell you: Love your enemies and pray for those who persecute you."
Matthew 5:43, 44*

What is the hardest thing to understand about these verses?

What is the most difficult part of living out the verses?

Stuff TO REMEMBER

Write down one thing you want to remember about today.

Today's date: _____

PRAYER STORY #2

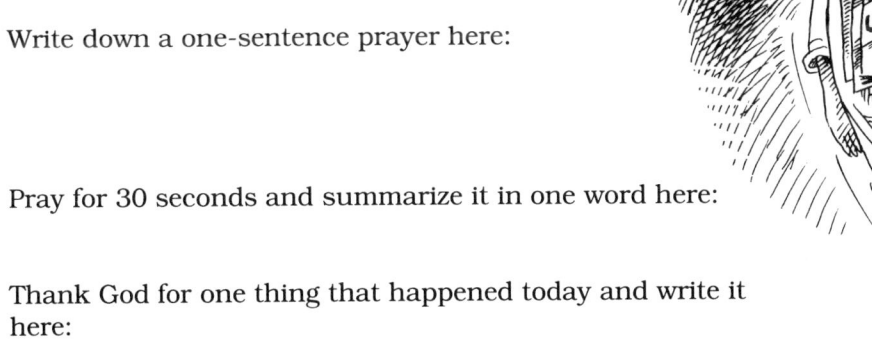

Have you ever shot up a quick prayer to God? Nehemiah did. You can read about his "prayer in a flash" in Nehemiah 2:1-5. It is good to be in the habit of prayer so that when you need a speedy prayer, you are prepared. Practice some short prayers below.

Write down a one-sentence prayer here:

Pray for 30 seconds and summarize it in one word here:

Thank God for one thing that happened today and write it here:

Tell God how you are feeling right now and write it here:

DATE COMPLETED: _____

EXTRA ☑ CREDIT

"In the same way, the Spirit helps us in our weakness. We do not know what we ought to pray for, but the Spirit himself intercedes for us with groans that words cannot express. And he who searches our hearts knows the mind of the Spirit, because the Spirit intercedes for the saints in accordance with God's will."
Romans 8:26, 27

How can these verses help you in your prayer life?

 TO REMEMBER

Write down one thing you want to remember about today.

Today's date: _____

TWENTY THREE

JESUS STORY #2

The prophet Isaiah gave a message of hope to all the nations of his time. The sermon described a coming Messiah. Read this prophecy about Jesus, delivered years before His birth in Isaiah 53:1-12.

God promised a coming Messiah—and He delivered. Write a paragraph about what Jesus Christ means to you. Use what you learned from Isaiah's prophecy as you write.

DATE COMPLETED: _____

E X T R A ☑ C R E D I T

"Who, being in very nature God, did not consider equality with God something to be grasped, but made himself nothing, taking the very nature of a servant, being made in human likeness. And being found in appearance as a man, he humbled himself and became obedient to death—even death on a cross!"
Philippians 2:6-8

Why was it important that Christ died for you?

 TO REMEMBER

Write down one thing you want to remember about today.

Today's date: _____

TWENTY FOUR

PRAYER STORY #3

The Bible tells that Daniel of the
Old Testament prayed regularly
every day. Read the story in
Daniel 6:10, then complete the
following sentences:

Having a daily time of prayer is
tough because . . .

The thing that keeps me from having a special time of daily prayer is . . .

I could discipline myself to be more like Daniel if . . .

DATE COMPLETED: _____

EXTRA ✔ CREDIT

"Evening, morning and noon I cry out in distress, and he hears my voice."
Psalm 55:17

*"Very early in the morning, while it was still dark, Jesus got up,
left the house and went off to a solitary place, where he prayed."*
Mark 1:35

How could a regular time of prayer help you grow in your relationship with Christ?

Stuff TO REMEMBER

Write down one thing you want to remember about today.

Today's date: _____

TWENTY FIVE

THE SERMON NOBODY WANTED TO HEAR

Near the end of the Old Testament is a book that contains some sermons that the people of Israel did not want to hear. The Jews had failed to care about the poor, the hurting, and the oppressed. The prophet Amos preached some burning messages to remind God's people of their forgetfulness. You can read them in the Book of Amos. The theme verse to read is Amos 5:24.

List five social problems you see in the world today (for example, the homeless, hunger):

1.

2.

3.

4.

5.

If you could work on any of these social problems, which one would you choose? Why?

DATE COMPLETED: _____

EXTRA  CREDIT

*"Learn to do right! Seek justice, encourage the oppressed.
Defend the cause of the fatherless, plead the case of the widow."*
Isaiah 1:17

Why is this verse so difficult to live out?

 TO REMEMBER

Write down one thing you want to remember about today.

Today's date: _____

RUNNING ON EMPTY

Have you ever run away from God? Jonah did (read Jonah 1:1-3) and we all know the end of that story. If you don't, you can find out by reading the rest of the Book of Jonah.

Make a list of all the things you believe God wants you to do but you haven't done:

_____

_____

_____

_____

_____

_____

_____

_____

_____

_____

_____

_____

What stands in the way of your doing these things for God?

Which thing(s) from your list do you have the courage to begin working on?

DATE COMPLETED: _____

E X T R A ☑ C R E D I T

"Where can I go from your Spirit? Where can I flee from your presence?
If I go up to the heavens, you are there; if I make my bed in the depths,
you are there. If I rise on the wings of the dawn, if I settle on the far side of
the sea, even there your hand will guide me, your right hand will hold me fast."
Psalm 139:7-10

What, to you, is the most comforting thing you learned from this passage?

Stuff TO REMEMBER

Write down one thing you want to remember about today.

Today's date: _____

TWENTY SEVEN

POPULAR PASSAGES #3

Read each of the Bible passages listed below. Choose the one that you feel would be the most helpful for you today.

- ❑ 1 Samuel 16:7
- ❑ Isaiah 26:3
- ❑ Romans 8:38, 39
- ❑ 2 Corinthians 1:3, 4
- ❑ Ephesians 4:32

Now that you've made a choice . . .

1. Pray that the Holy Spirit will speak to you as you study the passage.
2. Read the passage over three more times.
3. Decide what the author of the passage was trying to teach the readers of the time.
4. Determine how the passage applies to you.
5. Write down any changes you'll make because of what you learned from studying the passage.

DATE COMPLETED: _____

E X T R A  C R E D I T

*"I have hidden your word in my heart
that I might not sin against you."*
Psalm 119:11

How can learning and practicing what the Bible says protect you against sinning?

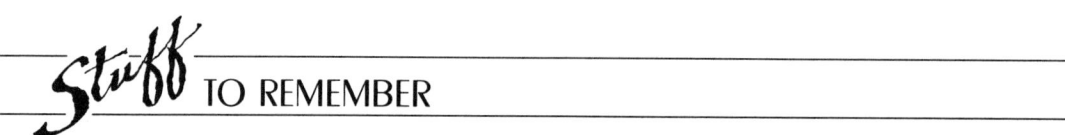 TO REMEMBER

Write down one thing you want to remember about today.

Today's date: _____

TWENTY EIGHT

THE DEVIL MADE ME DO IT

Read about the temptation of Christ in Matthew 4:1-11.

When are you tempted the most?

When are you tempted the least?

How did quoting Scriptures help Christ overcome temptation?

How could you use Scripture to overcome the temptations you face?

DATE COMPLETED: _____

EXTRA ✓ CREDIT

*"No temptation has seized you except what is common to man. And God is faithful;
he will not let you be tempted beyond what you can bear. But when you are tempted,
he will also provide a way out so that you can stand up under it."*
1 Corinthians 10:13

How do you look for ways out when you are tempted?

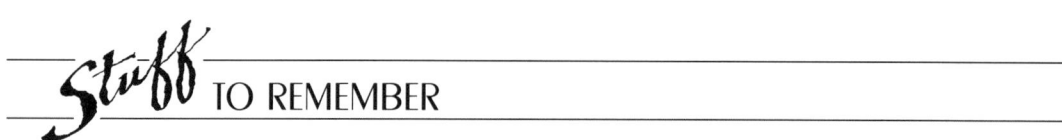

Stuff TO REMEMBER

Write down one thing you want to remember about today.

Today's date: _____

LIVING THE PSALMS #3

Do you want to focus your attention on
God? You can do this through praise.
Choose one of these psalms from
the list below. While you read it,
consider all that God has done.
Go ahead and appreciate God.

- Psalm 8
- Psalm 65
- Psalm 96
- Psalm 100
- Psalm 117
- Psalm 150

Write down some of the things you
appreciate about God that you read about
in this psalm.

DATE COMPLETED: _____

EXTRA ☑ CREDIT

"Through Jesus, therefore, let us continually offer to God a sacrifice of praise—the fruit of lips that confess his name. And do not forget to do good and to share with others, for with such sacrifices God is pleased."
Hebrews 13:15, 16

How can doing good and sharing with others in the name of Jesus be one way you can praise God?

 TO REMEMBER

Write down one thing you want to remember about today.

Today's date: _____

SMART BUILDING

Once upon a time there were two builders. You can read about them in Matthew 7:24-27.

Write a letter to Jesus that describes how you have put into practice what He taught in Matthew 7. (As a P.S., talk about what you still need to work on.)

DEAR JESUS,

P.S. LORD, I STILL NEED TO . . .

DATE COMPLETED: _____

EXTRA ✓ CREDIT

"All Scripture is God-breathed and is useful for teaching, rebuking, correcting and training in righteousness, so that the man of God may be thoroughly equipped for every good work."
2 Timothy 3:16, 17

How is the Bible useful to you?

 TO REMEMBER

Write down one thing you want to remember about today.

Today's date: _____

THIRTY ONE

HOW'S YOUR EYESIGHT?

Peter began to sink when he took his eyes off of Jesus. Read all about it in Matthew 14:22-33.

When is it easiest for you to take your eyes off of Jesus?

What do you usually do when you take your eyes off of Jesus?

What usually reminds you to keep your eyes on Jesus?

Why would you want to keep your eyes on Jesus?

I plan to keep my eyes on Jesus more consistently by . . .

DATE COMPLETED: _____

EXTRA ☑ CREDIT

"Let us fix our eyes on Jesus, the author and perfecter of our faith,
who for the joy set before him endured the cross, scorning its shame, and sat down
at the right hand of the throne of God. Consider him who endured such opposition
from sinful men, so that you will not grow weary and lose heart."
Hebrews 12:2, 3

How can reflecting on Christ's work on the cross strengthen your relationship with Him?

 TO REMEMBER

Write down one thing you want to remember about today.

Today's date: _____

THIRTY TWO

JESUS STORY #3

Jesus had taught His disciples that He was in fact the Savior, God's promised Messiah. This meant He was to die for their sins and on the third day rise again from the dead. But the disciples still didn't get it. The disciples had their own ideas about what a savior would do and those ideas did not include the Cross. They took for granted that their ideas of a savior were right. You can read the story in Matthew 16:21-23.

How do you take for granted what Christ has done for you on the cross?

How do you express your thanks to the Lord for what He has done for you on the cross?

DATE COMPLETED: _____

E X T R A  C R E D I T

"Then Jesus said to his disciples, 'If anyone would come after me,
he must deny himself and take up his cross and follow me.'"
Matthew 16:24

How are you living as one of Jesus' disciples?

 TO REMEMBER

Write down one thing you want to remember about today.

Today's date: _____

THIRTY THREE

JESUS HAD A LITTLE LAMB

Shepherds in the days of Jesus cared about their sheep. They knew each of the sheep in their herd individually. The sheep of ancient times needed constant protection and care. Thieves tried to steal them. Wild animals preyed upon them for food. Jesus told a short story in Matthew 18:12-14 in which He described God as an incredible shepherd.

Think back to a time when you were lost, really lost. Describe the worst thing about being lost.

Describe how you felt when you were found (or found your way back to the right place).

Now, describe how being "found" by Christ makes you feel.

DATE COMPLETED: _____

EXTRA ☑ CREDIT

"I am the good shepherd; I know my sheep and my sheep know me—just as the Father knows me and I know the Father—and I lay down my life for the sheep."
John 10:14

Describe how you feel knowing that Jesus is *your* good shepherd.

 **TO REMEMBER**

Write down one thing you want to remember about today.

Today's date: _____

THIRTY FOUR

PRAYER STORY #4

When is it the most difficult for you to pray?

When is it the easiest for you to pray?

Mark 14:32-42 describes Peter, James, and John faithfully praying with Jesus—uh, sort of. Read the story for yourself.

How does it feel to know that Jesus' disciples had trouble praying?

How is your prayer life like or unlike these three disciples' prayer life?

DATE COMPLETED: _____

EXTRA ✓ CREDIT

"And when you pray, do not keep on babbling like pagans, for they think they will be heard because of their many words. Do not be like them, for your Father knows what you need before you ask him."
Matthew 6:7, 8

Make a list of twenty things that need your prayers. Pray for each item one by one right now. Don't worry if your prayer is short. The length of your prayer is not as important as its content.

1.
2.
3.
4.
5.
6.
7.
8.
9.
10.

11.
12.
13.
14.
15.
16.
17.
18.
19.
20.

What did you learn by praying through the list you created?

How could a list like this help you discipline yourself to pray more?

 TO REMEMBER

Write down one thing you want to remember about today.

Today's date: _____

THIRTY FIVE

JESUS WHO?

Peter disowned Jesus.
You can read about his
denial in Mark 14:66-72.
He felt so bad that he
broke down and cried.

Choose the word or words from the list below that best describes how you might
feel if you denied knowing Christ.

Relieved	Free	Angry
Sad	Joyous	Guilty
Empty	Devastated	Hurt
Confused	Lonely	Happy
Comforted	Peaceful	Disappointed

DATE COMPLETED: _____

EXTRA ☑ CREDIT

"Yet at the same time many even among the leaders believed in him. But because of the Pharisees they would not confess their faith for fear they would be put out of the synagogue; for they loved praise from men more than praise from God."
John 12:42, 43

How can you live out your Christian faith without fear or shame?

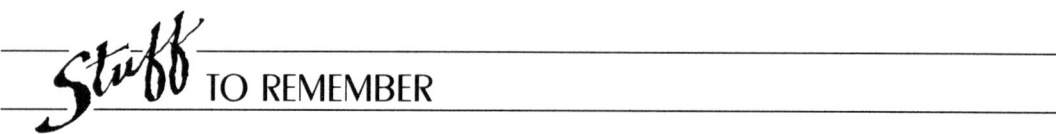

Stuff TO REMEMBER

Write down one thing you want to remember about today.

Today's date: _____

THIRTY◆SIX
GOOD SAM

The story of the good Samaritan is a tough story. You can read about it in Luke 10:25-37. This story told by Jesus raises some hard-to-answer questions. Answer them yourself, then ask an adult whom you respect and get his or her opinion.

How can you be responsible for yourself while helping others?

When is it not safe to help others?

With all the problems in the world, whom do you help first?

When is it appropriate not to help someone who is in need?

Who is your neighbor?

DATE COMPLETED: _____

E X T R A  C R E D I T

"Carry each other's burdens,
and in this way you will fulfill the law of Christ."
Galatians 6:2

I guess the best way to do what the above verse says is to . . .

 TO REMEMBER

Write down one thing you want to remember about today.

Today's date: _____

POPULAR PASSAGES #4

Read each of the passages listed below. Choose the one that you feel would be the most helpful for you today.

- ❑ Jeremiah 17:7, 8
- ❑ Romans 12:13
- ❑ Galatians 5:22, 23
- ❑ Philippians 4:6, 7
- ❑ James 4:7

Now that you've made a choice . . .

1. Pray that the Holy Spirit will speak to you as you study the passage.
2. Read the passage over three more times.
3. Decide what the author of the passage was trying to teach the readers of the time.
4. Determine how the passage applies to you.
5. Write down any changes you'll make because of what you learned from studying the passage.

DATE COMPLETED: _____

EXTRA  CREDIT

*"He replied, 'Blessed rather are those
who hear the word of God and obey it.'"*
Luke 11:28

Why might people who obey God's Word be happy (blessed)?

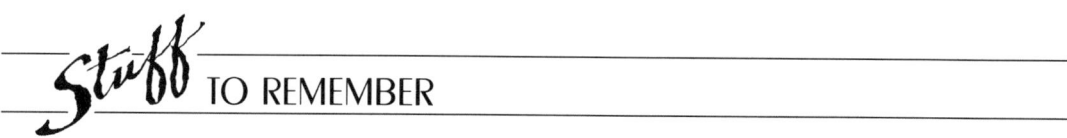 TO REMEMBER

Write down one thing you want to remember about today.

Today's date: _____

THIRTY EIGHT

A FOOL AND HIS MONEY

It's easy to get caught up in our materialistic culture. Jesus told a story of a certain rich man who became preoccupied with his wealth. You can read the parable in Luke 12:13-21.

Make a list of everything in your room. Beside each item write its approximate cost.

TOTAL AMOUNT
OF ROOM WEALTH = _____

How are you like or unlike the certain rich man in the story Jesus told?

DATE COMPLETED: _____

EXTRA ☑ CREDIT

*"No servant can serve two masters. Either he will hate the one
and love the other, or he will be devoted to the one and despise the other.
You cannot serve both God and Money."*
Luke 16:13

Whom or what do you serve the most?

What needs to change in your life in order for you to serve God more and other things less?

Stuff TO REMEMBER

Write down one thing you want to remember about today.

Today's date: _____

NIGHT QUEST

Nicodemus was on a spiritual journey. He was a religious leader at the time of Jesus' ministry on earth. He came to Christ with spiritual questions. You can read about his quest in John 3:1-21.

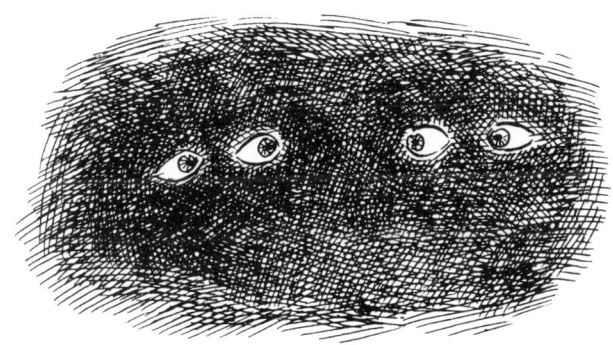

Like Nicodemus, you are on a spiritual journey. On the life line below, record five things that have happened to you in your relationship with God. These can be both positive and negative experiences. Write down your experiences on the five diagonal lines.

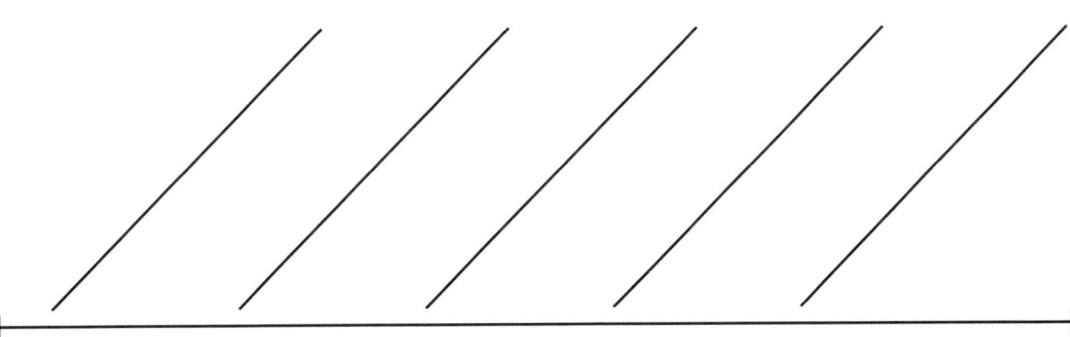

Year you
were born

Today's
date

DATE COMPLETED: _____

E X T R A ☑ C R E D I T

"For God so loved the world that he gave his one and only Son,
that whoever believes in him shall not perish but have eternal life."
John 3:16

What does this popular Bible passage mean in your life?

What does it mean in the life of your family? Your friends?

Stuff TO REMEMBER

Write down one thing you want to remember about today.

Today's date: _____

FORTY

LIVING THE PSALMS #4

A lot of people look at prayer as a chore, something that is really not much fun. Prayer is great fun! One way to make prayer fun is by praying one of the psalms. Practice doing this right now. Choose one of the psalms from the list below and read it as a prayer.

- Psalm 23 (Start with something like, "Lord, You are my shepherd . . ."
- Psalm 63
- Psalm 86
- Psalm 116
- Psalm 139

How did it feel to read the psalm as a prayer?

DATE COMPLETED: _____

EXTRA ☑ CREDIT

*"For we do not have a high priest who is unable to sympathize with our weaknesses,
but we have one who has been tempted in every way, just as we are—yet was
without sin. Let us then approach the throne of grace with confidence,
so that we may receive mercy and find grace to help us in our time of need."*
Hebrews 4:15, 16

How does this passage make your prayer life more meaningful?

 TO REMEMBER

Write down one thing you want to remember about today.

Today's date: _____

FORTY ONE

A FAMOUS DOUBTER

Doubts about God, about our Christian faith, about the Bible! All Christians have them. Are doubts bad? Not always. In fact, many times your doubts actually help strengthen your faith. Read about a famous doubter in John 20:24-29.

Write down five questions you have about the Christian faith.

1. _____ ?
2. _____ ?
3. _____ ?
4. _____ ?
5. _____ ?

How could you best get answers for these five questions? Do they need to be answered for you to keep your faith?

DATE COMPLETED: _____

E X T R A  C R E D I T

Read Psalm 13.

How can your questions help you grow in your faith in Christ?

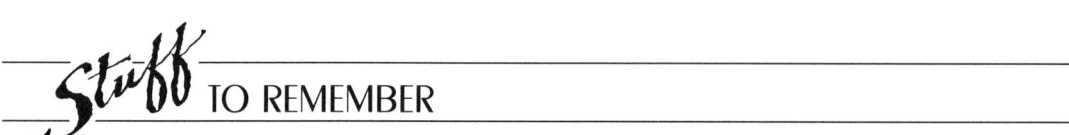 TO REMEMBER

Write down one thing you want to remember about today.

Today's date: _____

FORTY TWO

LET'S REVIEW #2

A Christian named Stephen defended himself against false accusations. He repeated a story of the history of the people of Israel and their relationship with God. The story painted a picture of divine love and deliverance even when God's people were not always faithful. Stephen's story is in Acts 7:2-50. The story ends with Jesus. The point of the story, and of the history of Israel, is Jesus, the ultimate in God's love and deliverance. Stephen ends his storytelling with some accusations of his own. Read them in Acts 7:51-53.

How are you sometimes stiff-necked?

How have you ignored the prophets of the Old Testament?

How have you not obeyed God's law?

How has God's love and deliverance been demonstrated in your life?

DATE COMPLETED: _____

EXTRA ☑ CREDIT

*"For everything that was written in the past was written to teach us,
so that through endurance and the encouragement
of the Scriptures we might have hope."*
Romans 15:4

How do the Old Testament Bible stories encourage you?

What hope do the Scriptures give you for your life?

Stuff TO REMEMBER

Write down one thing you want to remember about today.

Today's date: _____

FORTY•THREE
PERSECUTION PLUS

The Bible teaches that there will be persecution for those who follow Christ. You can read about the start of the promised persecution in Acts 8:1-4.

Write a letter to God, describing your feelings about being persecuted for Christ.

WHEN I THINK ABOUT BEING PERSECUTED BECAUSE I AM A CHRISTIAN, I . . .

ONE QUESTION I HAVE ABOUT PERSECUTION IS . . .

I WISH I COULD . . .

DATE COMPLETED: _____

EXTRA ☑ CREDIT

"Blessed are those who are persecuted because of righteousness, for theirs is the kingdom of heaven. Blessed are you when people insult you, persecute you and falsely say all kinds of evil against you because of me. Rejoice and be glad, because great is your reward in heaven, for in the same way they persecuted the prophets who were before you."
Matthew 5:10-12

How can you be happy even when you're persecuted by others because of your faith in Jesus Christ?

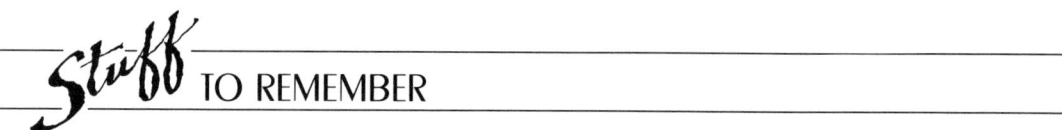 **Stuff** TO REMEMBER

Write down one thing you want to remember about today.

Today's date: _____

FORTY FOUR

POPULAR PASSAGES #5

Read each Bible passage listed below. Choose the one that you feel would be the most helpful for you today.

- ❑ Micah 6:8
- ❑ John 14:27
- ❑ Romans 13:14
- ❑ Philippians 1:6
- ❑ 2 Timothy 2:22

Now that you've made a choice . . .

1. Pray that the Holy Spirit will speak to you as you study the passage.
2. Read the passage over three more times.
3. Decide what the author of the passage was trying to teach the readers of the time.
4. Determine how the passage applies to you.
5. Write down any changes you'll make because of what you learned from studying the passage.

DATE COMPLETED: _____

EXTRA ✓ CREDIT

"The grass withers and the flowers fall, but the word of our God stands forever."
Isaiah 40:8

"Heaven and earth will pass away, but my words will never pass away."
Mark 13:31

How important is God's Word to you?

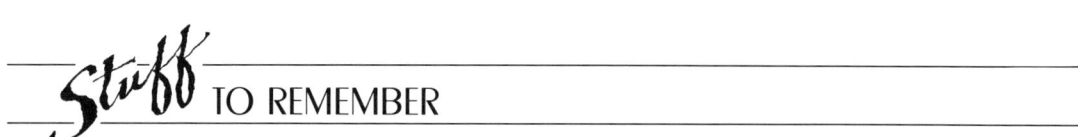 TO REMEMBER

Write down one thing you want to remember about today.

Today's date: _____

PROBLEM-FREE

Life's problems disappear when a person becomes a Christian. At least that is what some Christians think. But is this true or only a rumor? When Saul the unbeliever became Paul the Christian, did his problems disappear? You can read about his story in Acts 9:23-26.

Why do you think Paul continued to follow Christ in spite of the problems?

Look at the problems in your own life. Do you have more or less problems as a result of following Christ? Put an X on the line scale below that best represents your situation.

Christianity reduces   Christianity creates
life's problems   more problems in life

Why do you think God doesn't rescue Christians from the problems of life?

If becoming a Christian doesn't take away life's problems, what *does* Christianity do for a person's life?

DATE COMPLETED: _____

E X T R A  C R E D I T

"And we know that in all things God works for the good of those who love him, who have been called according to his purpose."
Romans 8:28

What does this passage have to say to you about the problems and troubles of this life?

 TO REMEMBER

Write down one thing you want to remember about today.

Today's date: _____

JESUS STORY #4

People who believed in Jesus did not keep His story a secret. The good news spread from Jerusalem to the ends of the world (see Acts 1:8). There are many stories in the New Testament of Christ's followers sharing the good news. Read one of them in Acts 10:39-43.

Write out a short paragraph that describes how you could share the story of Jesus with your friends.

DATE COMPLETED: _____

EXTRA ☑ CREDIT

"Therefore go and make disciples of all nations, baptizing them in the name of the Father and of the Son and of the Holy Spirit, and teaching them to obey everything I have commanded you. And surely I am with you always, to the very end of the age."
Matthew 28:19, 20

This passage of Scripture is called The Great Commission. What part can you play in fulfilling this great commission given by Jesus before He left the earth?

 TO REMEMBER

Write down one thing you want to remember about today.

Today's date: _____

GET RID OF THE "DIS" IN DISAGREEMENT

Disagreements are a part of everyday life. Being a Christian does not protect you from conflicts in relationships. Check out a disagreement the apostle Paul and other Christians had in the early church by reading Acts 15:35-40. Believe it or not, there were many disagreements among God's people.

What do you usually do when you have a disagreement with someone?

Describe a disagreement you experienced with a friend that didn't work out the way you had hoped.

Give a name that's a good description of the disagreement.

Now rewrite how the disagreement could have been handled in a positive way.

DATE COMPLETED: _____

EXTRA  CREDIT

"If it is possible, as far as it depends on you,
live at peace with everyone."
Romans 12:18

Brainstorm some positive ways you can handle disagreements you may face in the future.

Stuff TO REMEMBER

Write down one thing you want to remember about today.

Today's date: _____

FORTY◆EIGHT
IN LOVE WITH THE WORLD

Demas, an obscure figure in the New Testament, abandoned the apostle Paul. Why? Because . . . read about him in 2 Timothy 4:9, 10.

Make a list of all there is to love in this world.

How can you set your priorities so that the things you love in this world won't pull you away from following God?

DATE COMPLETED: _____

EXTRA ✓ CREDIT

"Do not love the world or anything in the world. If anyone loves the world, the love of the Father is not in him. For everything in the world—the cravings of sinful man, the lust of his eyes and the boasting of what he has and does—comes not from the Father but from the world. The world and its desires pass away, but the man who does the will of God lives forever."
1 John 2:15-17

How can you live in the world without becoming like the world?

 TO REMEMBER

Write down one thing you want to remember about today.

Today's date: _____

FORTY NINE

LET'S REVIEW #3

Read a famous repeat of Bible stories in Hebrews 11. The writer of Hebrews states that there is not enough time to review all the past heroes of the faith.

What do each of the Bible characters have in common?

What Bible character described in this Old Testament story repeat are you most like?

What does this repeat of Bible stories teach you about faith?

DATE COMPLETED: _____

EXTRA ☑ CREDIT

*"Therefore, since we are surrounded by such a great cloud of witnesses,
let us throw off everything that hinders and the sin that so easily entangles,
and let us run with perseverance the race marked out for us."*
Hebrews 12:1

Suppose these heavenly witnesses (those heroes of the faith mentioned in Hebrews 11) were watching you live the Christian life. How would your life compare to theirs?

How could their lives inspire yours?

What sins do you think easily entangle you?

Stuff TO REMEMBER

Write down one thing you want to remember about today.

Today's date: _____

FIFTY

A CHANGE OF HEART

Jude was the brother of Jesus Christ. During his brother's earthly stay, Jude did not seem to believe that Jesus was the Savior (see John 7:5). But Jude had a change of heart. He wrote a letter in the New Testament (read Jude, especially verses 3 and 4) where he warned Christians to watch out for false teachings. Jude moved from a nonbeliever to a defender of the faith. The Gospel had changed Jude.

Write a paragraph that describes how your relationship with Jesus Christ has changed you.

Write a paragraph that describes what Christ still needs to change in your life.

DATE COMPLETED: _____

E X T R A ☑ C R E D I T

"Therefore, my dear friends, as you have always obeyed—not only in my presence, but now much more in my absence—continue to work out your salvation with fear and trembling, for it is God who works in you to will and to act according to his good purpose."
Philippians 2:12, 13

This passage is not talking about earning your salvation. Rather it encourages you to get actively involved in growing as a Christian.

What part do you have in your growth as a Christian?

What part does God play?

Stuff TO REMEMBER

Write down one thing you want to remember about today.

Today's date: _____

FIFTY ONE

POPULAR PASSAGES #6

Read each of the Bible passages listed below. Choose the one that you feel would be the most helpful for you today.

- ❑ John 16:33
- ❑ Romans 12:9
- ❑ 1 Corinthians 10:31
- ❑ Galatians 2:20
- ❑ 1 Peter 5:7

Now that you've made a choice . . .

1. Pray that the Holy Spirit will speak to you as you study the passage.
2. Read the passage over three more times.
3. Decide what the author of the passage was trying to teach the readers of the time.
4. Determine how the passage applies to you.
5. Write down any changes you'll make because of what you learned from studying the passage.

DATE COMPLETED: _____

EXTRA ☑ CREDIT

"The law of the Lord is perfect, reviving the soul. The statutes of the Lord are trustworthy, making wise the simple. The precepts of the Lord are right, giving joy to the heart. The commands of the Lord are radiant, giving light to the eyes."
Psalm 19:7, 8

Complete this sentence: To me, the Word of the Lord (the Bible) is . . .

 TO REMEMBER

Write down one thing you want to remember about today.

Today's date: _____

FIFTY TWO

THE END

Have you ever read the last page of a book to see how it ends? God lets you do that with His book, the Bible. Before you look at how it all ends, though, remember what's between the beginning and the end. Throughout the Bible you find stories of real people with real problems. You read about their spiritual successes and failures. And most important of all, you see God's solution to sin, Jesus Christ.

Complete the following ten sentences to get a picture of how far you have come in the last year!

This year God has taught me . . .

I used to . . .

I know I have grown in my relationship with Jesus Christ because . . .

One thing that surprised me spiritually this past year was . . .

If I had the last year to do over again, I would . . .

Right now God and I are . . .

I am glad that . . .

I am most concerned about . . .

This next year I am committed to . . .

I plan to continue studying the Bible by . . .

DATE COMPLETED: _____

EXTRA ☑ CREDIT

"But the day of the Lord will come like a thief. The heavens will disappear with a roar; the elements will be destroyed by fire, and the earth and everything in it will be laid bare. Since everything will be destroyed in this way, what kind of people ought you to be? You ought to live holy and godly lives."
2 Peter 3:10, 11

What does this verse say to you as you end this Bible study?

Fill out the growth contract found on the next page.

Stuff TO REMEMBER

Write down one thing you want to remember about today.

Today's date: _____

MY GROWTH CONTRACT

I, _____ , do hereby agree to work toward the
following goal in my spiritual life. (Example: I will begin a new Bible study next week.)

I plan to reach my goal by doing the following things: (Example: Go to a Christian
bookstore and get a devotional book. Read the book every Tuesday and Thursday.)

I will know that I have reached my goal when I . . . (Example: When I have completed
reading the devotional book.)

If I fail to reach my goal by _____ , I will rewrite my contract
                                        (date)
and try again!

_____   _____
Signature   Date

MY GROWTH CONTRACT

I, _____, do hereby agree to work toward the following goal in my spiritual life. (Example: I will begin a new Bible study next week.)

I plan to reach my goal by doing the following things: (Example: Go to a Christian bookstore and get a devotional book. Read the book every Tuesday and Thursday.)

I will know that I have reached my goal when I . . . (Example: When I have completed reading the devotional book.)

If I fail to reach my goal by _____, I will again rewrite my
                                              (date)
contract and try, try again!

Signature   Date

116

MAJOR LIFE EVENTS

DATE

EVENT

MAJOR LIFE EVENTS

DATE   **EVENT**

MAJOR LIFE EVENTS

DATE   **EVENT**

MAJOR LIFE EVENTS

DATE   **EVENT**

MAJOR LIFE EVENTS

DATE   **EVENT**

_____   _____

_____   _____

_____   _____

_____   _____

_____   _____

_____   _____

_____   _____

_____   _____

_____   _____

_____   _____

_____   _____

_____   _____

_____   _____

_____   _____

_____   _____

_____   _____

_____   _____

_____   _____

_____   _____

_____   _____

_____   _____

_____   _____

PRAYER REQUESTS AND PRAISE

Date	Request	Praise

PRAYER REQUESTS AND PRAISE

DATE	REQUEST	PRAISE

PRAYER REQUESTS AND PRAISE

DATE	REQUEST	PRAISE

PRAYER REQUESTS AND PRAISE

Date	Request	Praise

PRAYER REQUESTS AND PRAISE

DATE	REQUEST	PRAISE